I'M FAST!

KATE & JIM McMULLAN

BALZER + BRAY
An Imprint of HarperCollinsPublishers

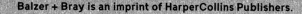

Balzer + Bray is an imprint of HarperCollins Publishers.

I'm Fast! Text copyright © 2012 by Kate McMullan Illustrations copyright © 2012 by Jim McMullan All rights reserved. Manufactured in China. No part of this book may be used or reproduced in any manner whatsoever without written permission except in the case of brief quotations embodied in critical articles and reviews. For information address HarperCollins Children's Books, a division of HarperCollins Publishers, 10 East 53rd Street, New York, NY 10022. www.harpercollinschildrens.com

Library of Congress Cataloging-in-Publication Data.
McMullan, Kate.
    I'm fast! / by Kate & Jim McMullan. — 1st ed.
        p.   cm.
    Summary: A train and a car race each other to Chicago.
    ISBN 978-0-06-192085-1 (trade bdg.) — ISBN 978-0-06-192086-8 (lib. bdg.)
    [1. Railroad trains—Fiction.   2. Racing—Fiction.]   I. McMullan, Jim, ill.   II. Title.
III. Title: I am fast!
PZ7.M47879Il   2012   2010013669
[E]—dc22

12 13 14 15 16   SCP   10 9 8 7 6 5 4 3 2 1 ❖ First Edition

For Anika & Carter Petruccelli

Thanks to the HarperCollins crew, Alessandra Balzer, Ruiko Tokunaga, Sara Sargent, Jenny Rozbruch, Carla Weise, and Kathryn Silsand, for keeping us ON TRACK, and a big TOOO-OOOO to Holly McGhee, Joan Slattery, and Elena Mechlin over at Pippin.

What's that, Red?
You wanna have a RACE?
Vrrrrrrrrrrr-rum!
First one to Chicago wins?
You're on!
Lemme load my FREIGHT.

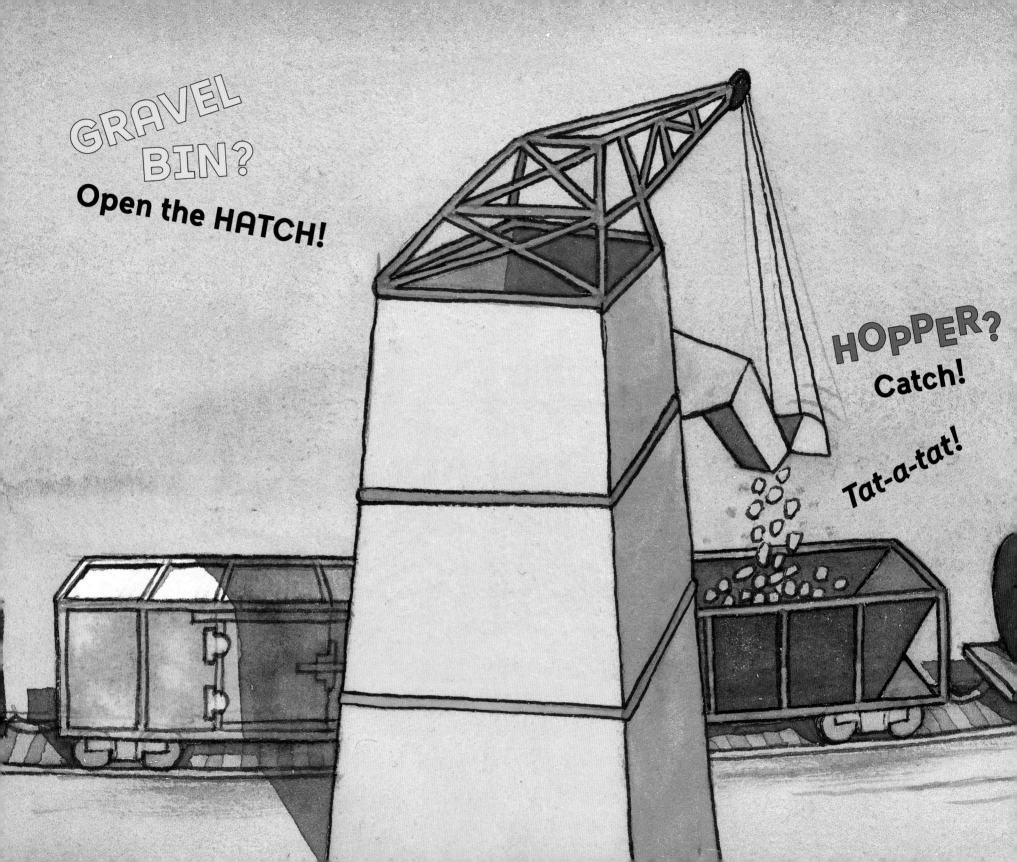

I'm haulin' a
FREEZER CAR full of
ICE-CREAM BARS!
Gotta get 'em to Chicago
ICY COLD!

Chooka chooka

chooka chooka

MOUNTAIN ahead!
CARS on my AUTO-RACK,
DUCK!

Takin' a shortcut
through the ROCK—

TOOOOOOOOOO-OO

Chooka chooka chooka chooka chooka

FULL SPEED AHEAD
through the tunnel—

TOOOOOOOOO!

Chooka chooka chooka chooka

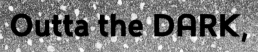

Outta the DARK,
into the—

SNOW!

So? **PLOW** right through it.

Car? Can't do it—
Nothin' to it for a

FREIGHT TRAIN!
Choo-ka Choo-ka Choo-ka Choo-ka

I'm EATIN' UP track!

Got a BOXCAR
filled with BOXES—
filled with WHEAT, EGGS,
TOMATOES, PEPPERS,

CHEESE!

WONDER
WHEAT

EXCELLENT
EGGS

TERRIFIC
TOMATOES

Chooka chooka chooka chooka

WHEELS on the RAILS, ALL night long,
Racin' and a-rumblin' the
FREIGHT TRAIN song—
Chooka chooka chooka chooka

Towin' TRUCKS—
STACKED PIGGYBACK!
TRUCKERS tucked inside
their cabs
SLEEP LIKE BABIES!

Shhhhhhhhh!

Chooka chooka chooka chooka

TOOOOOOOO-OO-OOOOOO!

Cows? You gotta *MOOOOOOOOVE* it!

Thanks, ladies!

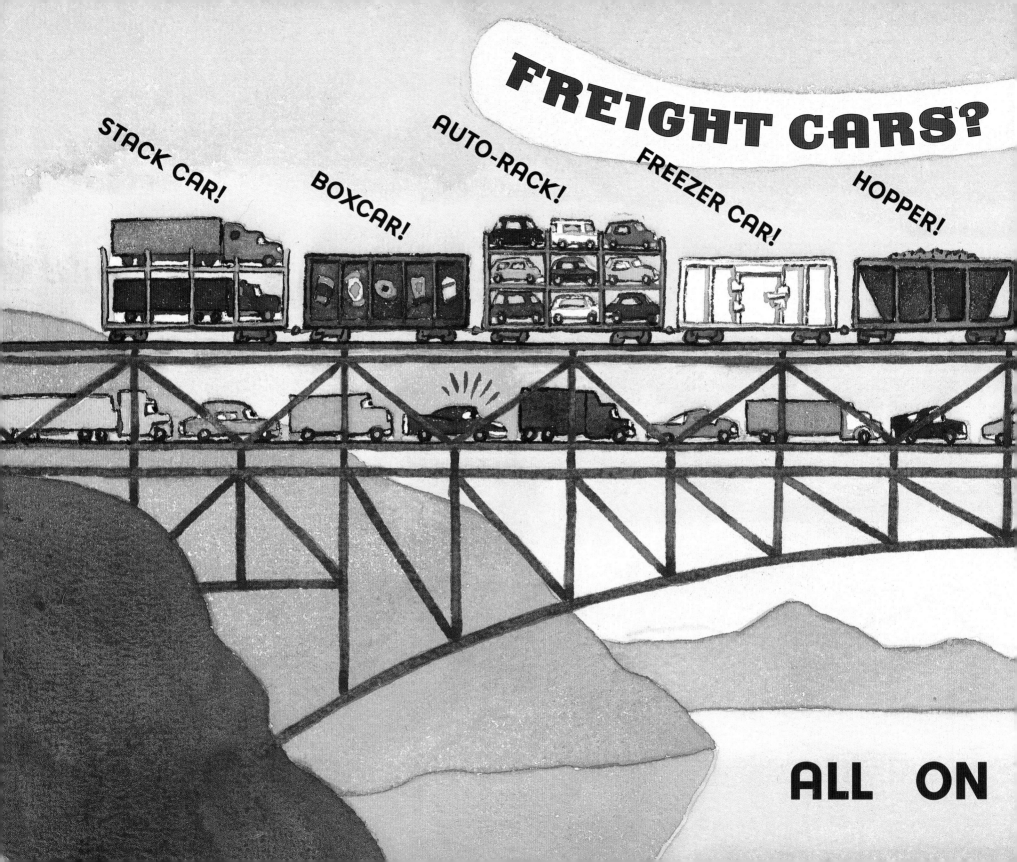

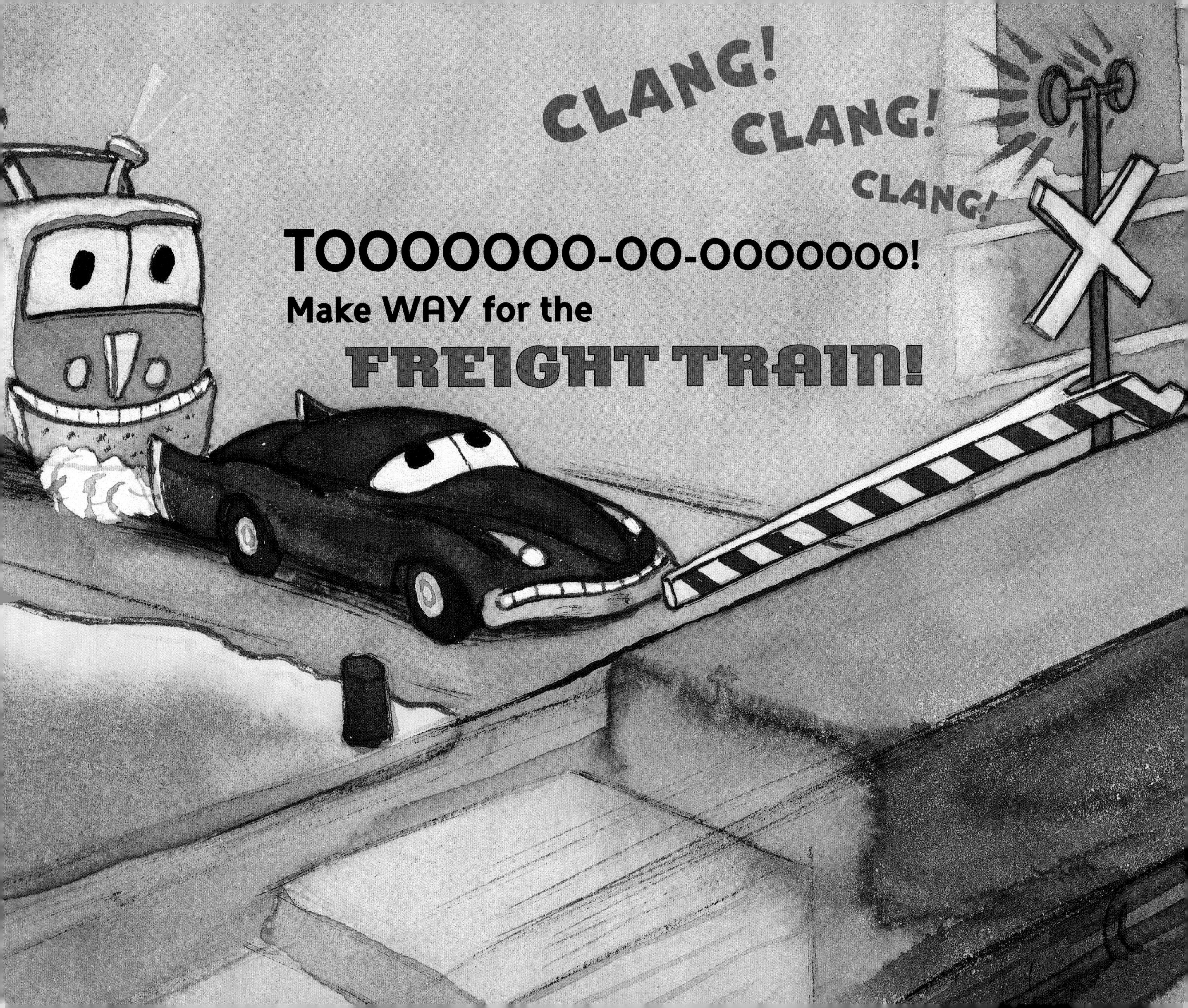

TOOOOOOO-OO-OOOOOOOO!
Make WAY for the
FREIGHT TRAIN!

Onto the SIDE TRACK, THROTTLE BACK.

Won the race to Chicago—

YESSSSSSSSSSSSSSSSSSSSSSSSSS!

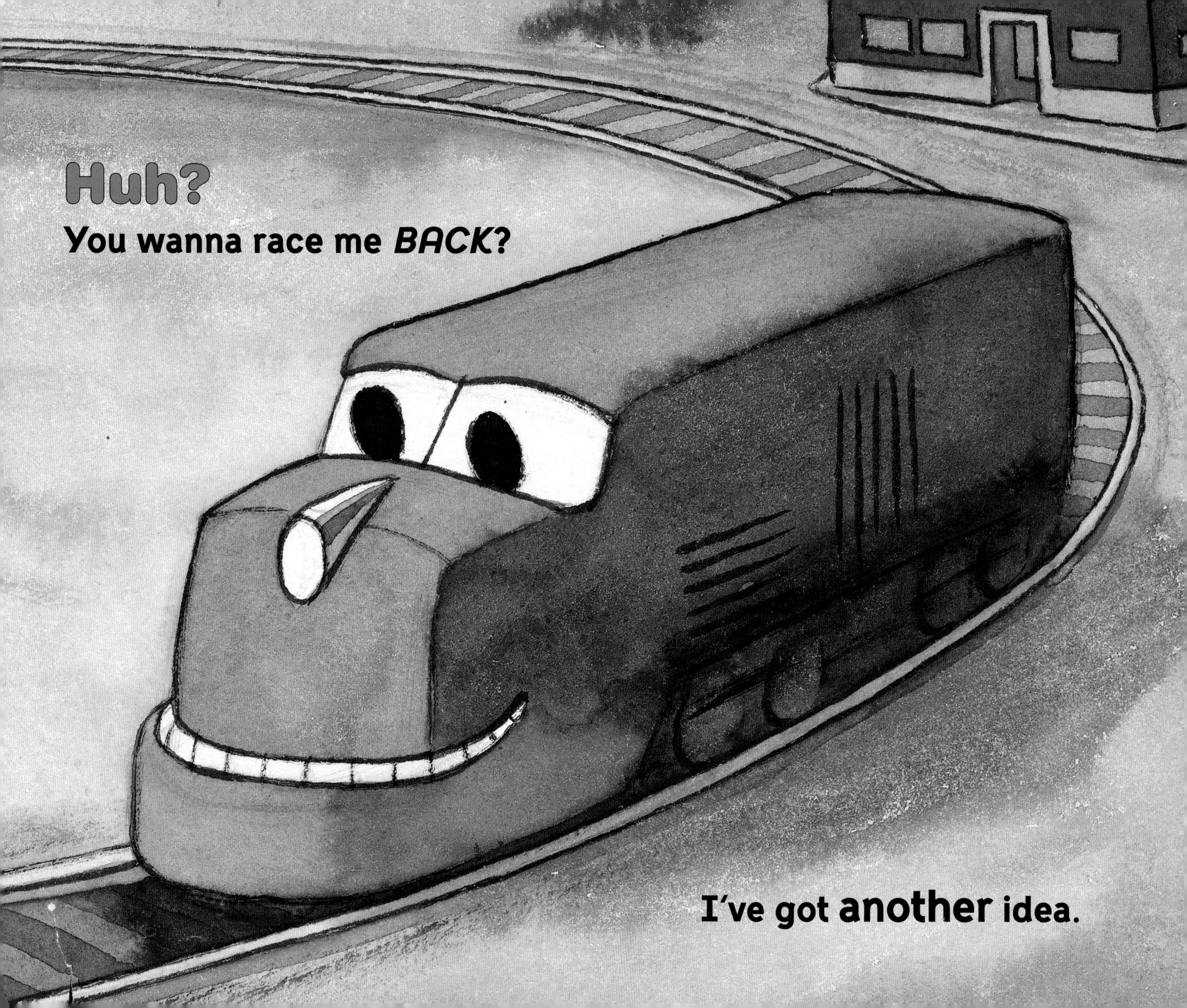

Huh?

You wanna race me *BACK*?

I've got another idea.

Take the **TRAIN**, Red!
Yeah, roll on up!
I'll get you there—
FAST!